Practis[e]
Cursive
Writing

Colour each picture as you finish each page.

Written by Jillian Harker and Geraldine Taylor
Illustrated by Andrew Everitt-Stewart
Calligraphy by Maureen Hallahan

Ladybird

Letter formation

Copy these letters.

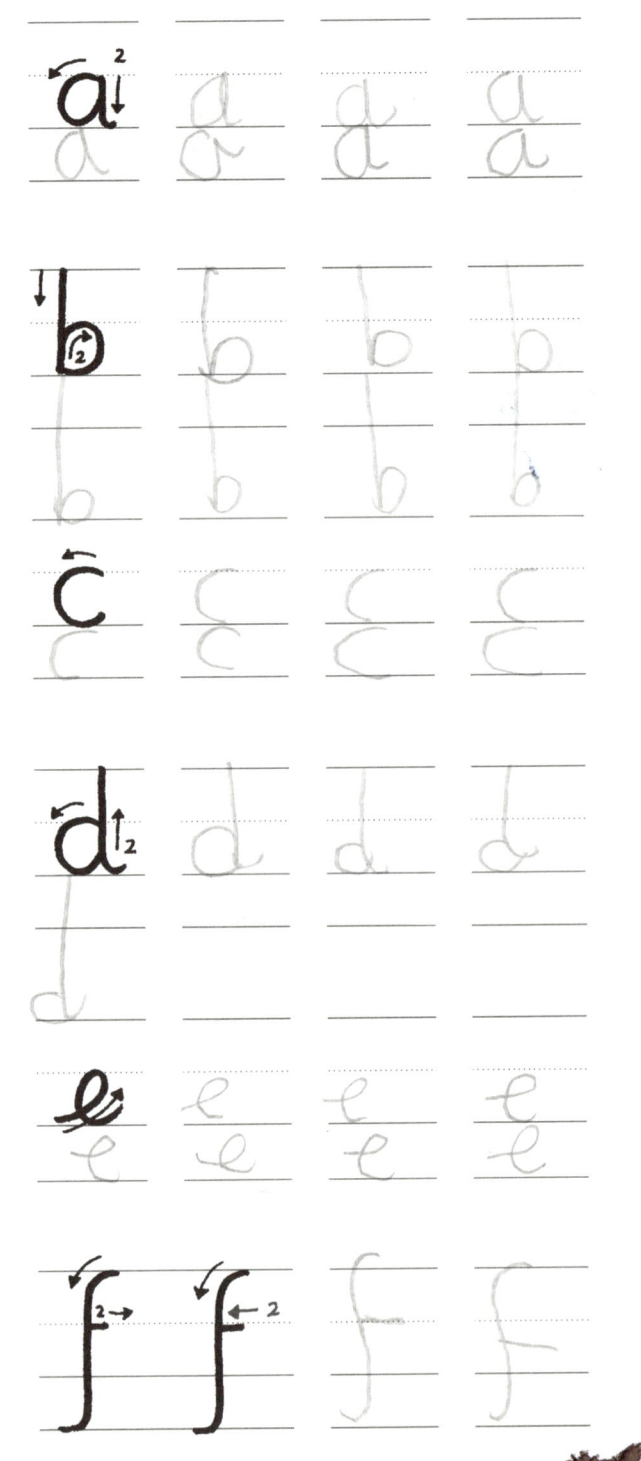

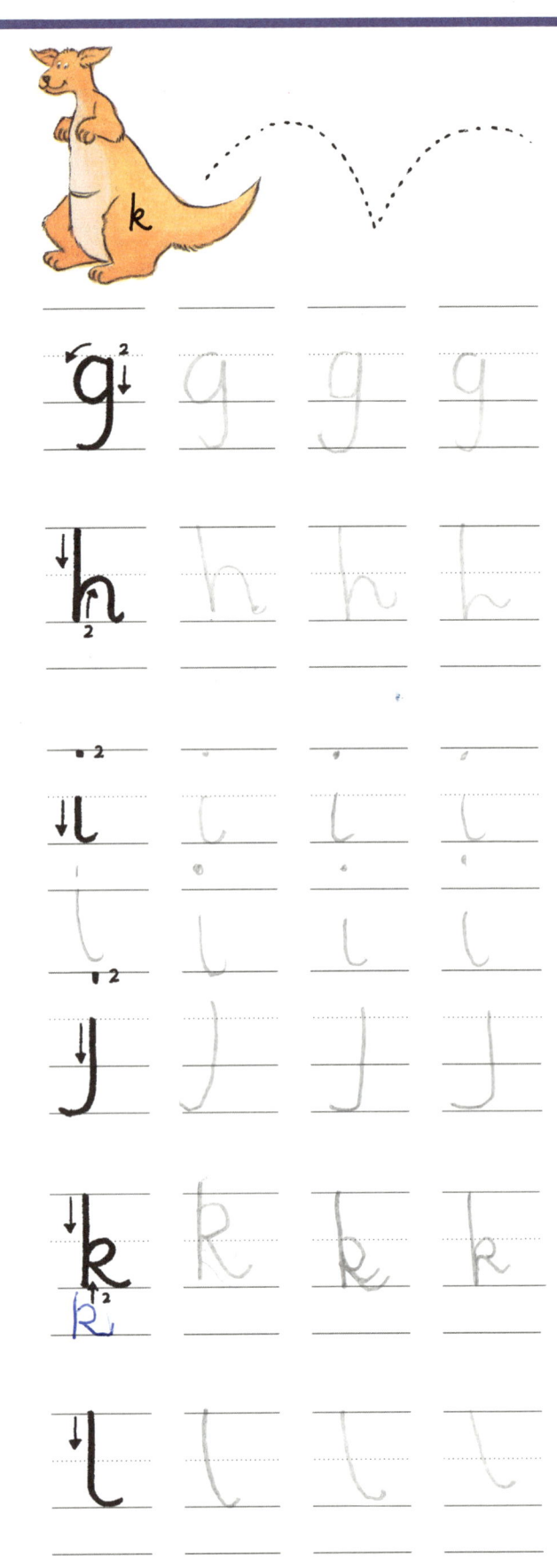

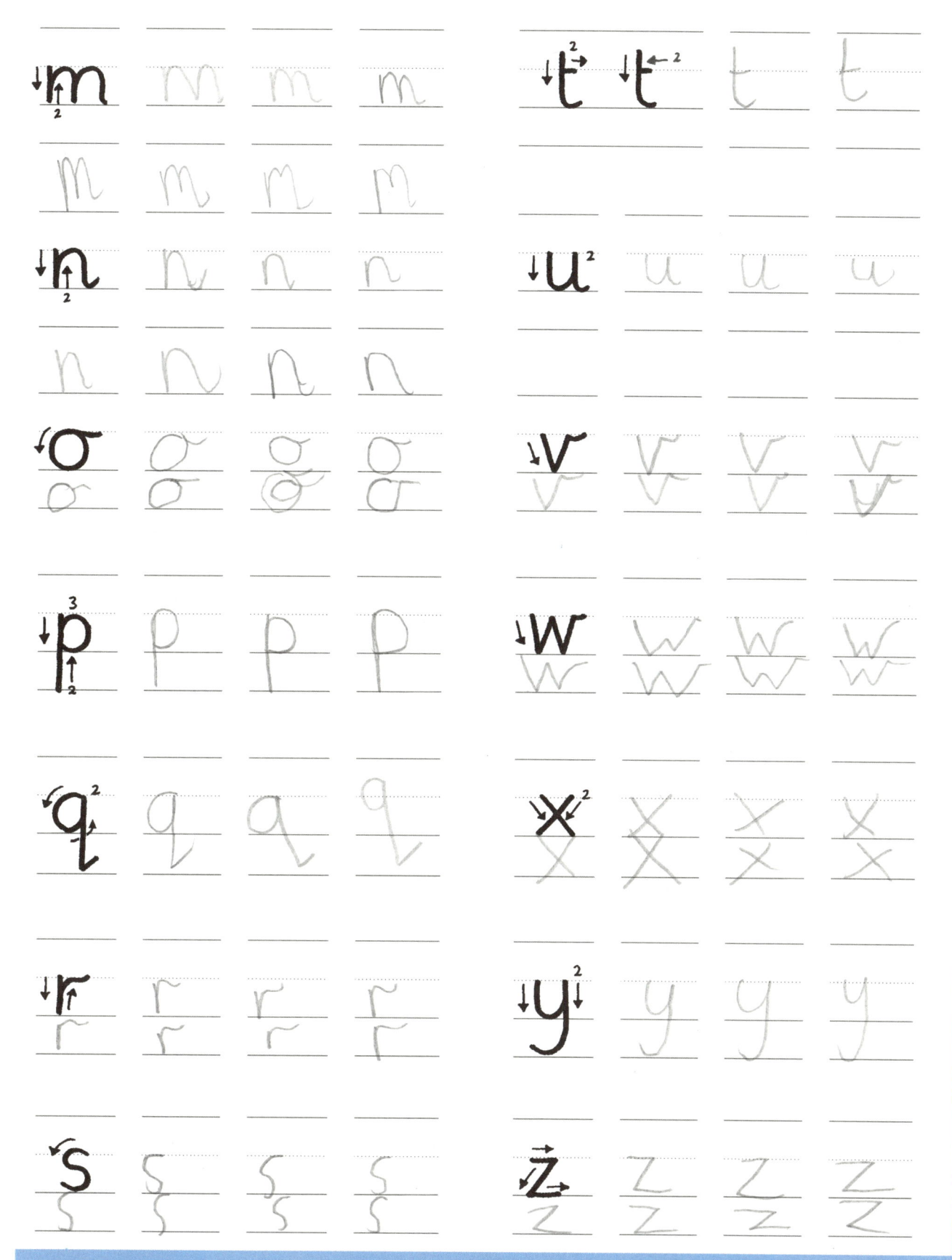

Parent point: By the time your child starts school, you will know if she* is right or left-handed. You will make it easier for a left-hander if you show how to form certain letters of the alphabet her special way. Left-handers should look for the grey arrows on these pages. Keep plenty of spare paper handy for extra practice. For all children, correct letter formation from the very beginning is the foundation for good handwriting.

*The child is referred to as she throughout this book; activities are equally suitable for boys and girls.

Capital letter formation

Copy these letters.

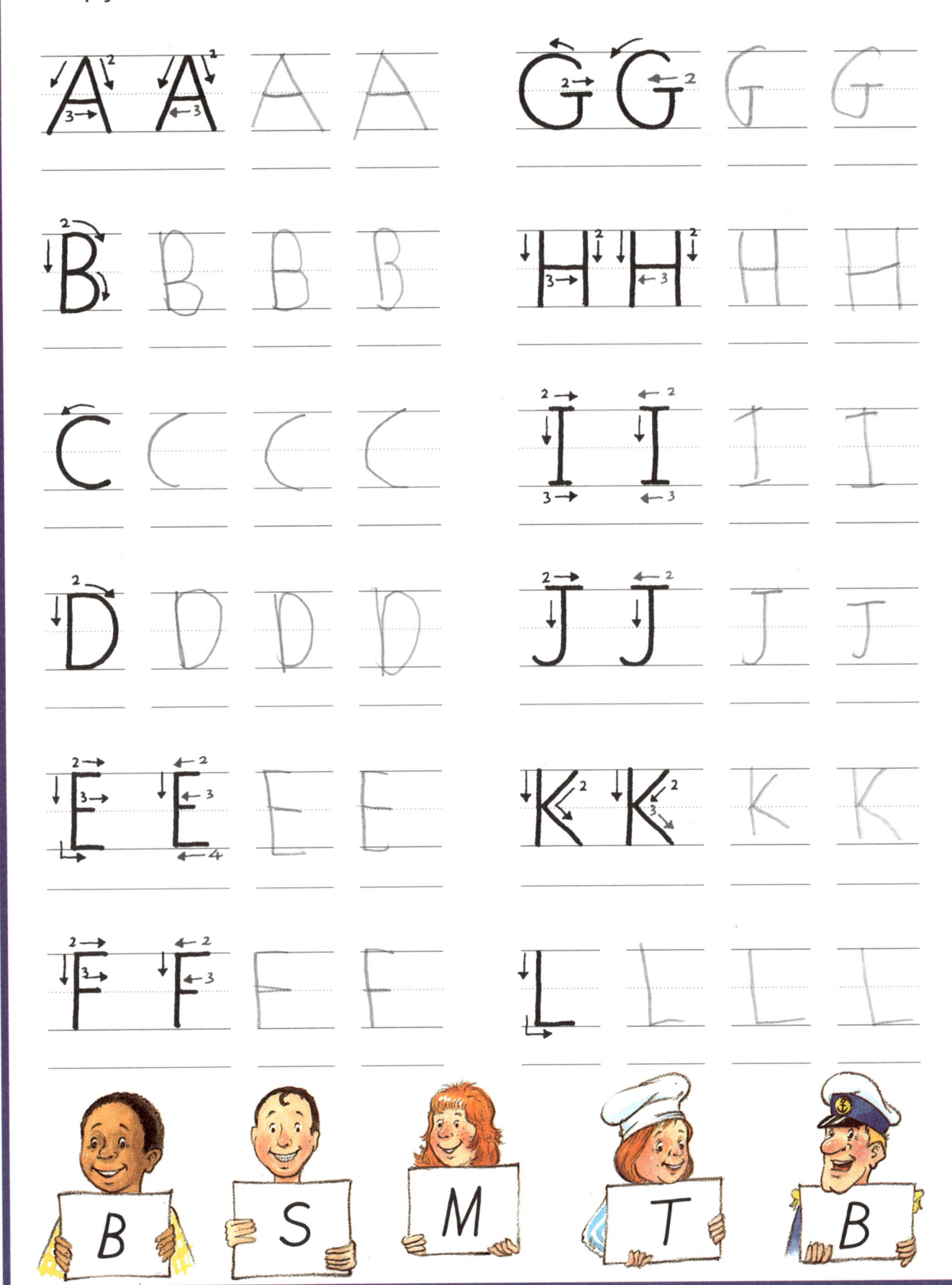

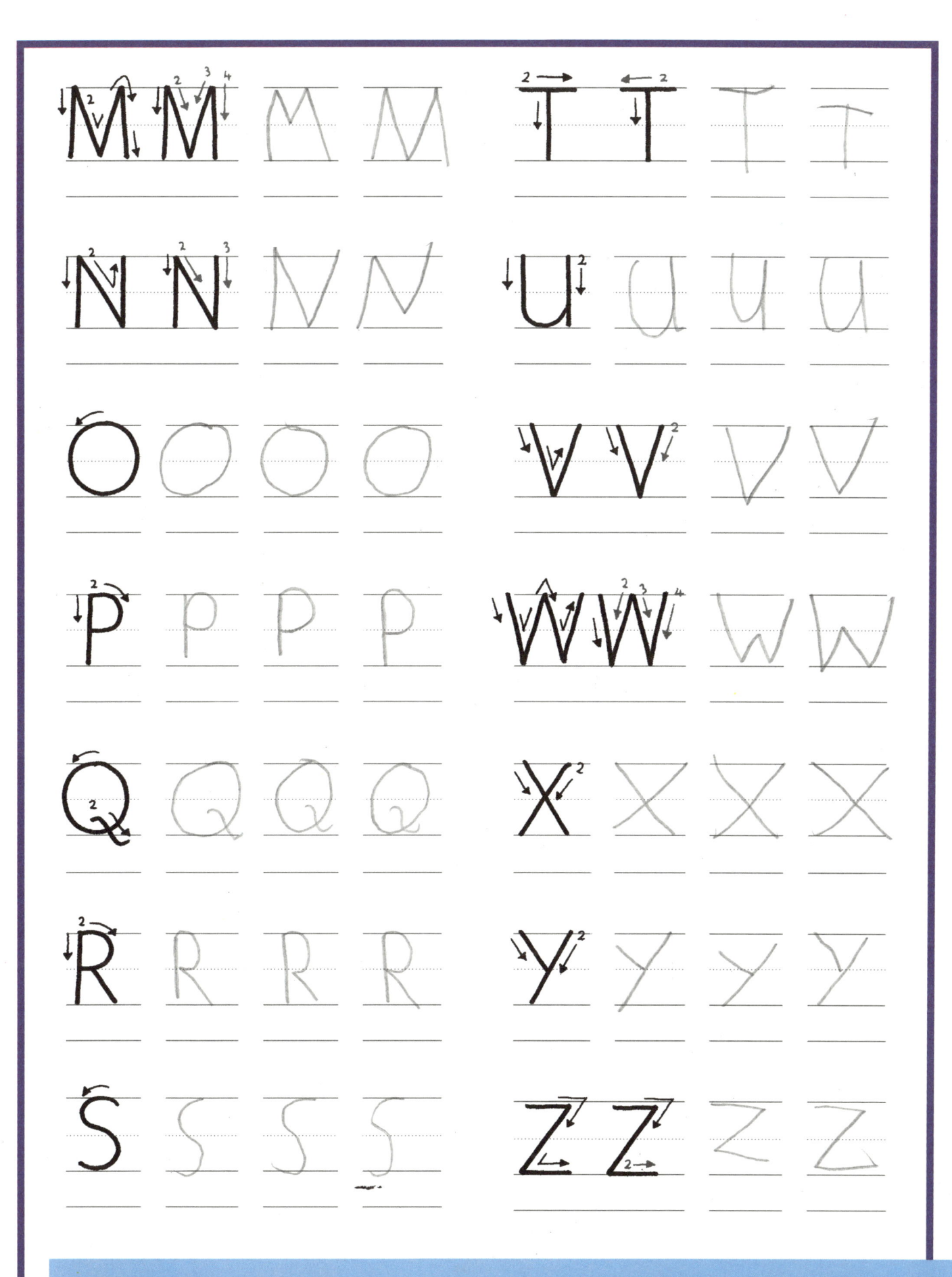

Parent point: You will make it easier for a left-hander if you show your child how to form certain letters of the alphabet her special way. Left-handers should look out for the grey arrows on some of the capital letters.

For all children, correct letter formation from the very beginning is the foundation for good handwriting.

Labelling maps

His crew shout and yell and give him a shake
But nothing they do can make Pirate Snore wake.

Practise each word, or part of a word, so that you can help Pirate Snore find the treasure.

an	fin
pan	en
sand	den
land	ten
bank	on
sank	pond
in	

While Pirate Snore was asleep, one of his crew rubbed out some of the words on his treasure map. Choose the words from the lists and write them back in the correct place on the map.

ship _sank_ here

shark's _fin_

ten trees

small _pond_

ten ✓
land ✓
sand ✓
sank ✓

yellow _sand_

dragon's _den_

den ✓
fin ✓
pond ✓
bank ✓

land here   steep _bank_

Choose the correct word to write what the pirate crew are doing.

drink   plan   sing

The pirates _plan_

The pirates _drink_

The pirates _sing_

Use your skills

On a piece of paper draw and label your own treasure map.

Parent point: Make sure your child is sitting at the correct height for the table. If necessary, use a cushion.

Writing speech

If your tap is broken, with lots of drips and drops
And if you need a plumber, then send for Mrs Stops.

Practise each word so that you can help Mrs Stops.

get			stop		
jog			drip		
dog			up		
job			tap		
pop			six		
mop			fix		
shop					

Help Mrs Stops tell you how she spends her day.
Fill in the missing words.

get
six

I _get_ up at _six_.

jog
dog

I _jog_ with my _dog_.

fix tap

I _fix_ tap.

I _pop_ into the _shop_.

job

I drive to the _job_.

pop
shop

stop drip

I _stop_ the _drip_.

mop up

I _mop_ _up_.

Use your skills

Write something you have done today.

Today I _went to a party._
It was fun

Parent point: The more varied opportunities you can provide for your child to practise handwriting, the more rewarding it will be. Writing speech in speech balloons is exciting for children.

Instructions

Bring all your animals along to see the vet
You will find out what to do from kindly Mr Pet.

Practise each word so that you can help Mr Pet tell people how to look after their animals.

cat	keep
rat	sheep
bat	sleep
dog	needs
frog	

Mr Pet has started to write some instructions for looking after the animals. Can you copy the words and help him to complete the instructions?

keep   *sleep*   *needs*

__keep__ warm   let __sleep__   __needs__ food

Mr Pet has lots of books to tell you how to look after your pet. Can you write the animal's name on its book?

How to look after your __frog__

How to look after your __cat__

How to look after your __sheep__

How to look after your __dog__

How to look after your __bat__

Use your skills

Ask a grown-up to help you make your own book about the animals you like.
Write the names of the animals on the book cover.

__guinea pigs__
__rabbits__
__and much more__

Parent point: Make sure your child is holding the paper steady with the hand that is not writing.

Rhymes and messages

"I'm the fastest sailor that ever sailed the sea."
Captain Boast cries out, "You won't catch me."

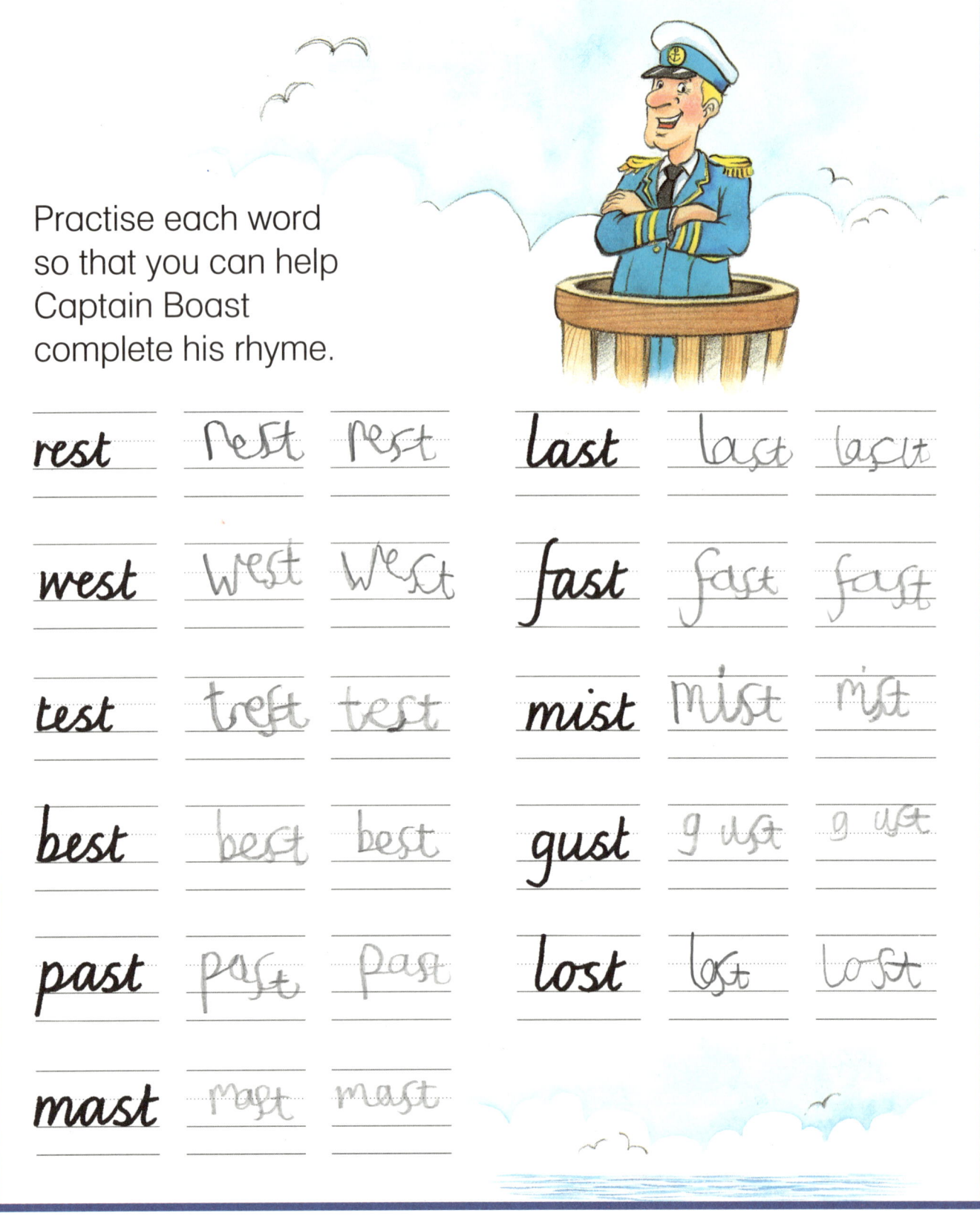

Practise each word so that you can help Captain Boast complete his rhyme.

rest	rest rest	last	last last
west	west west	fast	fast fast
test	test test	mist	mist mist
best	best best	gust	gust gust
past	past past	lost	lost lost
mast	mast mast		

Captain Boast is having a race. Copy the words to complete his rhyme.

best	I am the very ___best___
test	I pass every ___test___
rest	I never take a ___rest___
west	I sail from east to ___west___
mast	I climb up the ___mast___
past	When other ships go ___past___
last	I tell them they'll be ___last___
fast	Because I go so ___fast___ !

Copy the correct words to say why he does not win.

~~gust~~   ~~mist~~   ~~lost~~

Captain Boast met a ___gust___ of wind.

Captain Boast met ___mist___.   Captain Boast got ___lost___.

Use your skills

Write a message, asking for help, that Captain Boast can put in a bottle.

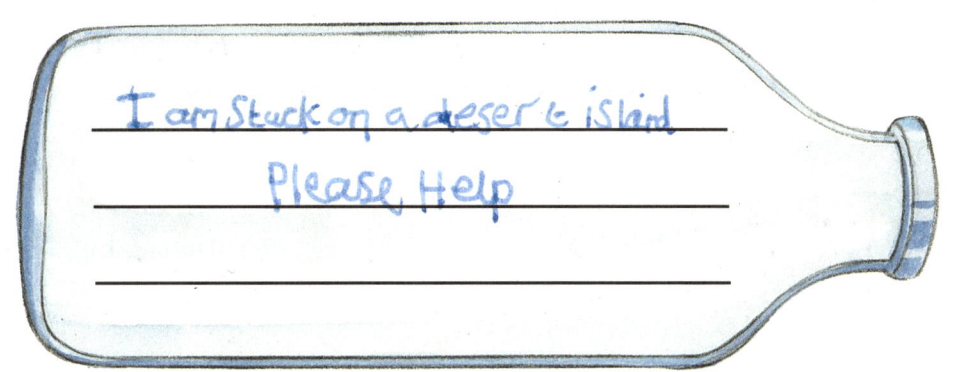

I am stuck on a desert island
Please Help

Parent point: Encourage your child to hold the pencil in a relaxed way between thumb and forefinger, supported on the middle finger.

Captions and advertisements

If you see a flash of silver in the night sky
It may be Mrs Starlight flying by.

Practise each word, or part of a word, so that you can help Mrs Starlight with her rocket adventures.

one	one	one one	rose	rose	rose rose
zone	zone	zone	ole	ole	ole ole
ome	ome	ome ome	pole	pole	pole pole
home	home	home	oke	oke	oke oke
ove	ove	ove ove	woke	woke	woke woke
drove	drove drove		smoke		smoke
ose	ose	ose ose	clothes		clothes

14

Mrs Starlight is writing a book about her flight. Can you write the correct word in each space to complete the captions?

① clothes

Put on space _clothes_

② zone

Went to takeoff _zone_

③ rose

Rocket _____ into sky

④ Smoke

_____ from booster rockets

⑤ Pole

Over South _____

⑥ Woke

_____ up among stars

⑦ Drove

_____ around planets

⑧ home

Back _____

Mrs Starlight writes lots of books. Can you complete these titles for her?

Alone   pole

Home   jokes

Lunar Bookshop
Books by Mrs Starlight

_____ in space

_____ from the sky

Above the _____

Star _____

Parent point: Use extra paper to practise the words on page 14. Encourage your child to write captions for her own pictures and to have fun designing and writing advertisements.

Songs

Mr Bang the builder is busy all day long
If you pass close by, you'll hear him sing his song.

Practise each word so that you can help Mr Bang write the words of his song.

hitting	pushed
fitting	pulled
sitting	fetched
cutting	fixed
planning	mixed
dropping	mended

Mr Bang likes to sing as he works.
Write the words to complete his song.

planning
cutting   I'm _____, _____

hitting
dropping   I'm _____, _____

fitting
sitting   I'm __Fitting__, __sitting__.

pushed
pulled   I've _____ and _____

fetched
fixed   I've _____ and _____

mended
mixed   I've _____ and _____.

Parent point: Use extra paper to practise the words on page 16. Make sure the elbow of your child's writing arm is in a relaxed position – not too far away from the body.

Book titles

In Miss Check's classroom you'll find a book
That's just right for you if you just take a look.

Practise each word so that you can help Miss Check with her books.

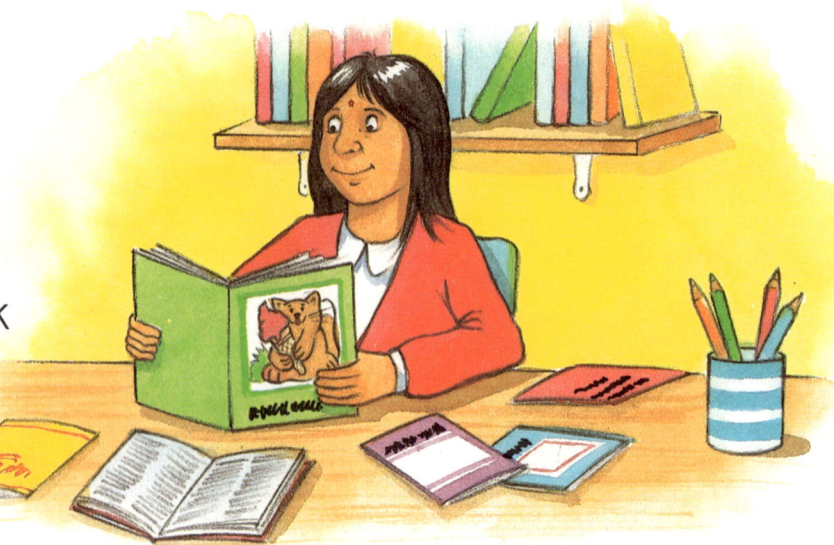

girl

circle

birds

birthday

over

river

letter

winter

silver

spider

All the children in Miss Check's class have been writing books. They have drawn the pictures for the covers. Can you help them with the titles?

The Silver Spider
Birds in winter
A birthday letter
Girl in a circle
Over the river

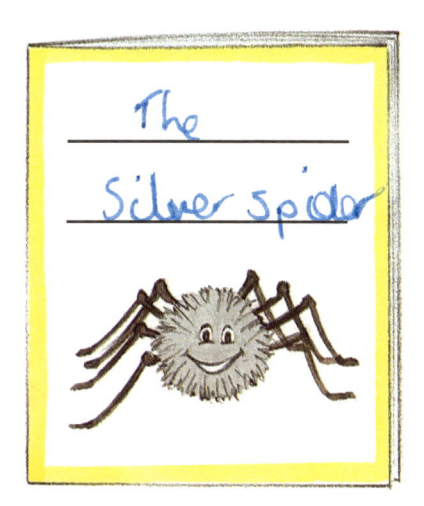

Use your skills

Can you think of a good title for this book about the dirty monster?
Write it on the book cover.

Parent point: Use extra paper to practise the words on page 18. Writing their own books for others to read is a highly rewarding activity for children.

Writing letters

Mr Breeze the beekeeper likes to show his bees
You can come and visit him near the nine pine trees.

Practise each word so that you can help Mr Breeze complete his letter.

nine

pine

prize

hive

arrive

live

time

like

write

white

invite

inside

Mr Breeze wants to invite the school children to visit. Help him to write the letter. Copy each word into the correct space.

like
invite
hives
prize
inside
white
hives
live
nine
Pine
write
time
arrive

9 Pine Tree Lane

Dear Miss Check

I would ____ to _____ your class to come and see my bee _____. The class will see the _____ honey the bees make _____ the ____ ____.

I ____ at number ____, ____ Tree Lane. Will you ____ to tell me the ____ you will ____?

Mr Breeze

Use your skills

Ask a grown up to help you write a letter to invite a friend to your house.

Parent point: Developing handwriting skills needs lots of concentration and stamina. Your understanding and encouragement are vital.

Posters

When Mr Smile the acrobat comes cycling into town
He likes to play the clown as he rides up and down.

Practise each word so that you can help Mr Smile with his poster.

side

ride

likes

smile

quite

seat

treat

ease

please

leaps

Mr Smile has to practise for his show and he has not had time to finish his poster. Please help him by copying the poem in the middle of the poster.

Mr Smile leaps with ease
Mr Smile likes to please
Take a seat
For quite a treat
And see him ride
From side to side!

Use your skills

Would you and your friends like to put on a show? Design a poster for your own show.

Parent point: When children know their handwriting will be displayed they are encouraged to do their best.

Diaries

Mr Harvest likes everything to be right
So he works on his farm from morning to night.

Practise each word so that you can help Mr Harvest to write his diary.

more

store

born

corn

morning

stormy

order

forget

fork

sort

north

important

Mr Harvest has been so busy looking after the new foal that he has not had time to write his diary. Can you write this for him?

Sort important jobs

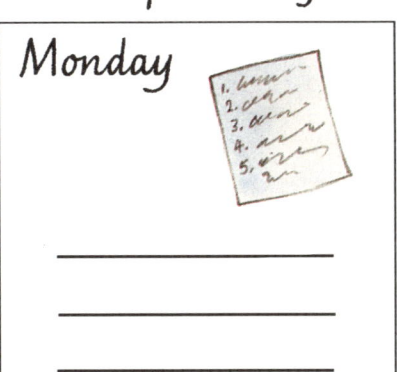

Monday

Stormy night with north wind

Tuesday

Check winter store

Wednesday

Order more feed

Thursday

Must not forget to mend fork

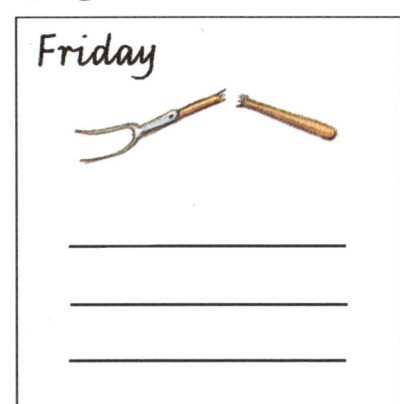

Friday

Cut corn

Saturday

New foal in the morning

Sunday

Use your skills

Ask a grown-up to help you write your own diary for a week and draw the pictures.

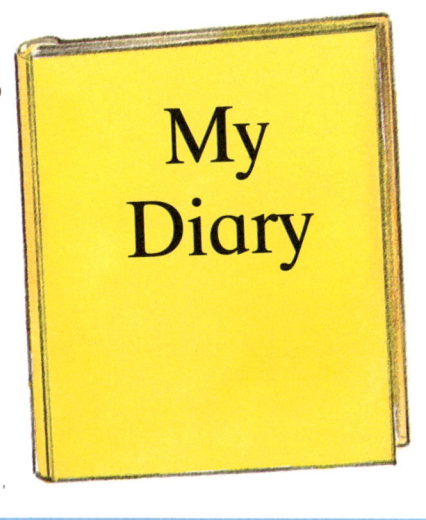

My Diary

Parent point: Use extra paper to practise the words on page 24. Encourage short, regular sessions of handwriting practice. Writing a diary is a good way of ensuring daily practice.

Notes and menus

Mrs Taste says, "Come and try
My cheese flan, chips and cherry pie."

Practise each word so that you can help Mrs Taste plan her cooking.

chop   cherry

chill   kitchen

cheese   fish

chips   dishes

lunch   finish

fetch   mash

chicken   sharp

Mrs Taste has pinned some notes around the kitchen to help her remember what to do. Write in the words she has forgotten.

fetch
| _____ vegetables |

bunch
| wash _____ of carrots |

sharp
| get _____ knife |

chop
| _____ onions |

fish
| cook _____ |

finish
| _____ laying table |

chill
| _____ drinks |

mash
| _____ potatoes |

dishes
| wash _____ |

kitchen
| clean _____ |

Use your skills

Write a menu for your favourite meal.
Ask a grown-up to help you list the words you need.

Parent point: Take advantage of all the opportunities for writing that arise naturally in a family context.

Notices and signs

Mrs Mow's garden shop opens every day
She has pretty plants to sell, and flowers on display.

Practise each word, or part of a word, so that you can help Mrs Mow in her garden shop.

ar

car

card

park

sharp

garden

ay

pay

way

trays

spray

today

Can you help Mrs Mow write some signs for her garden shop? Copy each word onto the correct sign.

park

car _____

cards

_____
for sale

today

open
_____ at

garden

_____ sprays

way

tools this _____

display

house plant
_____

trays

seed _____

sharp

_____
cutters

Use your skills

Draw a picture of Mrs Mow's shop.
Remember to write some signs.

Parent point: Use extra paper to practise the words on page 28. Writing their own signs and notices helps children to understand how important writing is in the world around them.

Stories

Mrs Track explores places far away
New people to see and adventures every day.

Practise each word so that you can help Mrs Track to write her story.

pack

truck

over

river

stormy

morning

forgot

important

rain

mountain

arrive

time

Mrs Track has come to talk to the children in Miss Check's class. She is telling them a story about her adventures. Can you write the story, using some of the words you have practised?

_____

_____

_____

_____

_____

_____

_____

_____

Use your skills

You could use your best handwriting to make your own book of rhymes. Draw a picture of each person you have met in this book, and copy out the rhyme that goes with each person.

Parent point: Use extra paper to practise the words on page 30. Pin up your child's stories for all the family to enjoy.

The alphabet

A a   B b   C c   D d

E e   F f   G g   H h

I i   J j   K k   L l

M m   N n   O o   P p

Q q   R r   S s   T t

U u   V v   W w   X x

Y y   Z z